TEEANTONETTE PRESENTS

DREAM BIG

BY JEDONNA MATHIS AND ZAMYAH ALBERT

ILLUSTRATED BY NAVI' ROBINS

JeDonna's Acknowledgement

First and foremost, I would like to thank God for blessing me with the gift to write. I would like to thank TeeAntonette Presents for the opportunity of adding me to their writing family. Thank you to Navi Robins for the wonderful illustrations. I want to give a huge thank you to my daughter ZaMyah for being my co-author and motivation to keep writing. She truly inspires me to strive for better. Thank you to all the people who support me and push me to keeping going. Thanks to my family and friends who support me thru everything. To all the children that may lay eyes on this book I appreciate you! Continue to use your imagination and don't be afraid to think the impossible! Always Dream Big! I love you all!

Sitting in my backyard wishing I had a big space ship to fly to the stars.

I close my eyes real tight, and imagine me on the moon and jumping over stars. Skipping from planet to planet, Pluto was small so I had to move slow so I didn't fall off.

Dream big momma always say so I have big dreams everyday.

Being in the lead during the race car derby, standing high with the trophy.

I picture myself swimming with the dolphins in the ocean.

fighting the bad guy trying to take over.

Having a big horse and being the best cowboy in the West.

Riding a dinosaur to school instead of the school bus.

I even have big dreams
while I'm sleeping.

Beating the dragon to help the princess and then be coming king.

Riding the clouds and flying with the birds.

Dreaming is fun, just close your eyes and imagine what you want.